DISCARD

It's Library Day

Janet Morgan Stoeke

• Dutton Children's Books •

Jennifer Gaines likes to read about trains.

And she smiles when she hears that it's library day.

And he smiles when he hears that it's library day.

Uma Rasheed has just learned to read.

And she smiles when she hears that it's library day.

They walk down the hall in a nice, neat line. The principal says they are doing just fine.

Miss Faye, the new librarian, loves to see the kids come in.

She finds each one the perfect book, because she knows just where to look.

But best of all, they sit on the floor and hear a story . . .

that makes them roar!

"Thank you, Miss Faye," the children all say.

And they can't wait until the next library day!

For David Lane

DUTTON CHILDREN'S BOOKS
A division of Penguin Young Readers Group

Published by the Penguin Group
Penguin Group (USA) Inc., 375 Hudson Street, New York, New York 10014, U.S.A.
Penguin Group (Canada), 90 Eglinton Avenue East, Suite 700, Toronto, Ontario,
Canada M4P 2Y3 (a division of Pearson Penguin Canada Inc.) • Penguin Books Ltd,
80 Strand, London WC2R 0RL, England • Penguin Ireland, 25 St Stephen's Green,
Dublin 2, Ireland (a division of Penguin Books Ltd) • Penguin Group (Australia),
250 Camberwell Road, Camberwell, Victoria 3124, Australia (a division of Pearson
Australia Group Pty Ltd) • Penguin Books India Pvt Ltd, 11 Community Centre,
Panchsheel Park, New Delhi - 110 017, India • Penguin Group (NZ), 67 Apollo
Drive, Rosedale, North Shore 0632, New Zealand (a division of Pearson
New Zealand Ltd) • Penguin Books (South Africa) (Pty) Ltd, 24 Sturdee
Avenue, Rosebank, Johannesburg 2196, South Africa • Penguin Books Ltd,
Registered Offices: 80 Strand, London WC2R 0RL, England

Copyright © 2008 by Janet Morgan Stoeke
All rights reserved.

LIBRARY OF CONGRESS CATALOGING-IN-PUBLICATION DATA

Stoeke, Janet Morgan.
It's library day / Janet Morgan Stoeke.—1st ed.   p. cm.
Summary: The children all walk down the hall in a nice straight line
and big grins on their faces since today is library day.
ISBN 978-0-525-47944-4 (hardcover)
[1. Stories in rhyme. 2. Books and reading—Fiction.
3. Libraries—Fiction.] I. Title. II. Title: It is library day.
PZ8.3.S86835It 2008   [E]—dc22   2007040589

Published in the United States by Dutton Children's Books,
a division of Penguin Young Readers Group
345 Hudson Street, New York, New York 10014
www.penguin.com/youngreaders

Designed by Abby Kuperstock

Manufactured in China • First Edition
1 3 5 7 9 10 8 6 4 2

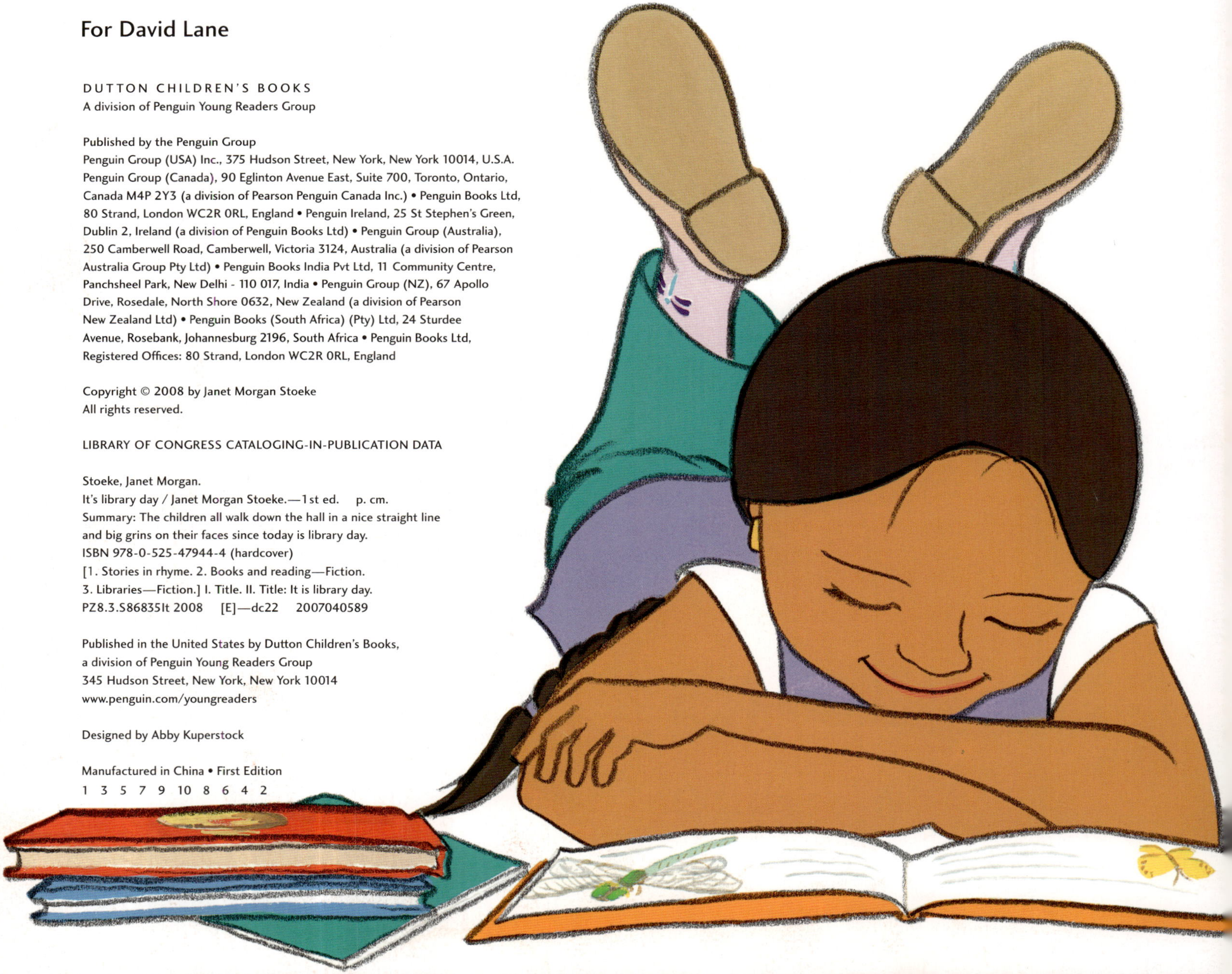